TWENTY-TWO

BY

MARY
ROBERTS
RINEHART

BLACKBIRD BOOKS
NEW YORK • LOS ANGELES

A Blackbird Classic, September 2023

Manufactured in the United States of America.

The events and characters depicted in this book are
fictional.

Cataloging-in-Publication Data

Rinehart, Mary Roberts.
Twenty-two / Mary Roberts Rinehart.
p. cm.
1. Romance fiction, American.
2. Medical personnel—Fiction.
3. Quarantine—Fiction. I. Title.
PS3535.I73 T84 2023 813'.54—dc23 2023939627

Blackbird Books
www.bbirdbooks.com
email us at editor@bbirdbooks.com

ISBN 978-1-61053-022-4

First Blackbird Edition

10 9 8 7 6 5 4 3 2 1

TWENTY-TWO

I

The Probationer's name was really Nella Jane Brown, but she was entered in the training school as N. Jane Brown. However, she meant when she was accepted to be plain Jane Brown. Not, of course, that she could ever be really plain.

People on the outside of hospitals have a curious theory about nurses, especially if they are under twenty. They believe that they have been disappointed in love. They never think that they may intend to study medicine later on, or that they may think nursing is a good and honorable career, or that they may really like to care for the sick.

The man in this story had the theory very hard.

When he opened his eyes after the wall of the warehouse dropped, N. Jane Brown was sitting beside him. She had been practicing counting pulses on him, and her eyes were slightly upturned and very earnest.

There was a strong odor of burnt rags in the air, and the man sniffed. Then he put a hand to his upper lip—the right hand. She was holding his left.

"Did I lose anything besides this?" he inquired. His little moustache was almost entirely gone. A gust of fire had accompanied the wall.

"Your eyebrows," said Jane Brown.

The man—he was as young for a man as Jane Brown was for a nurse—the man lay quite still for a moment. Then:

"I'm sorry to undeceive you," he said. "But my right leg is off."

He said it lightly, because that is the way he took things. But he had a strange singing in his ears.

"I'm afraid it's broken. But you still have it." She smiled. She had a very friendly smile. "Have you any pain anywhere?"

He was terribly afraid she would go away and leave him, so, although he was quite comfortable, owing to a hypodermic he had had, he groaned slightly. He was, at that time, not particularly interested in Jane

Brown, but he did not want to be alone. He closed his eyes and said feebly, "Water!"

She gave him a teaspoonful, bending over him and being careful not to spill it down his neck. Her uniform crackled when she moved. It had rather too much starch in it.

The man, whose name was Middleton, closed his eyes. Owing to the morphine, he had at least a hundred things he wished to discuss. The trouble was to fix on one out of the lot.

"I feel like a bit of conversation," he observed. "How about you?"

Then he saw that she was busy again. She held an old-fashioned hunting-case watch in her hand, and her eyes were fixed on his chest. At each rise and fall of the coverlet, her lips moved. Mr. Middleton, who was feeling wonderful, experimented. He drew four very rapid breaths, and four very slow ones. He was rewarded by seeing her rush to a table and write something on a sheet of yellow paper.

"Resparation, very iregular," was what she wrote. She was not a particularly good speller.

After that, Mr. Middleton slept for what he felt was a day and a night. It was really ten minutes by the hunting-case watch. Just long enough for the Senior Surgical Intern, known in the school as the

S.S.I., to wander in, feel his pulse, approve of Jane Brown, and go out.

Jane Brown had risen nervously when he came in and had proffered him the order book and a clean towel, as she had been instructed. He had, however, required neither. He glanced over the record, changed the spelling of "resparation," arranged his tie at the mirror, took another look at Jane Brown, and went out. He had not spoken.

It was when his white-linen clad figure went out that Middleton wakened and found it was the same day. He felt at once like conversation, and he began immediately. But the morphine did a curious thing to him. He was never afterward able to explain it. It made him create.

He lay there and invented for Jane Brown a fictitious person, who was himself. This person, he said, was a newspaper reporter, who had been sent to report the warehouse fire. He had got too close, and a wall had come down on him. He invented the newspaper, too, but, as Jane Brown had come from somewhere else, she did not notice this.

In fact, after a time he felt that she was not as really interested as she might have been, so he introduced a love element. He was, as has been said, of those who believe that nurses go into hospitals because of being blighted. So he introduced a Mabel, suppressing her other name, and boasted, in a way he afterward remembered with horror, that Mabel was in love with him. She was, he related, something or other on his paper.

At the end of two hours of babbling, a businesslike person in a cap—the Probationer wears no cap—relieved Jane Brown, and spilled some beef tea down his neck.

Now, Mr. Middleton knew no one in that city. He had been motoring through, and he had, on seeing the warehouse burning, abandoned his machine for a closer view. He had left it with the engine running, and, as a matter of fact, it ran for four hours, when it died of starvation, and was subsequently interred in a city garage. However, he owned a number of cars, so he wasted no thought on that one. He was a great deal more worried about his eyebrows, and, naturally, about his leg.

When he had been in the hospital ten hours it occurred to him to notify his family. But he put it off for two reasons: first, it would be a lot of trouble; second, he had no reason to think they particularly wanted to know. They all had such a lot of things to do, such as bridge and opening country houses and going to the Springs. They were really overwhelmed, without anything new, and they had never been awfully interested in him anyhow.

He was not at all bitter about it.

That night, Mr. Middleton—but he was now officially Twenty-two, by that system of metonymy which designates a hospital private patient by the number of his room—that night, Twenty-two had rather a bad time, between his leg and his conscience. Both carried on disgracefully. His leg stabbed, and his conscience reminded him of Mabel, and that if one is going to lie, there should at least be a reason. To lie out of the whole cloth!

However, toward morning, with what he felt was the entire pharmacopoeia inside him, and his tongue feeling like a tar roof, he made up his mind to stick to his story, at least as far as the young lady with the old-fashioned watch was concerned. He had a sort of creed, which shows how young he was, that one should never explain to a girl.

There was another reason still. There had been a faint sparkle in the eyes of the young lady with the watch while he was lying to her. He felt that she was seeing him in heroic guise, and the thought pleased him. It was novel.

To tell the truth, he had been getting awfully bored with himself since he left college. Everything he tried to do, somebody else could do so much better. And he comforted himself with this, that he would have been a journalist if he could, or at least have published a newspaper. He knew what was wrong with about a hundred newspapers.

He decided to confess about Mabel, but to hold fast to journalism. Then he lay in bed and watched for the Probationer to come back.

However, here things began to go wrong. He did not see Jane Brown again. There were day nurses and night nurses and reliefs, and Interns and Staff and the Head Nurse and the First Assistant and—everything but Jane Brown. And at last he inquired for her.

"The first day I was in here," he said to Miss Willoughby, "there was a little girl here without a cap. I don't know her name. But I haven't seen her since."

Miss Willoughby, who, if she had been disappointed in love, had certainly had time to forget it, Miss Willoughby reflected.

"Without a cap? Then it was only one of the probationers."

"You don't remember which one?"

But she only observed that probationers were always coming and going, and it wasn't worth while learning their names until they were accepted. And that, anyhow, probationers should never be sent to private patients, who are paying a lot and want the best.

"Really," she added, "I don't know what the school is coming to. Since this war in Europe every girl wants to wear a uniform and be ready to go to the front if we have trouble. All sorts of silly children are applying. We have one now, on this very floor, not a day over nineteen."

"Who is she?" asked Middleton. He felt that this was the one. She was so exactly the sort Miss Willoughby would object to.

"Jane Brown," snapped Miss Willoughby. "A little, namby-pamby, mush-and-milk creature, afraid of her own shadow."

Now, Jane Brown, at that particular moment, was sitting in her little room in the dormitory, with the old watch ticking on the stand so she would not overstay her off duty. She was aching with fatigue from her head, with its smooth and shiny hair, to her feet, which were in a bowl of witch hazel and hot water. And she was crying over a letter she was writing.

Jane Brown had just come from her first death. It had taken place in H ward, where she daily washed windowsills, and disinfected stands, and carried dishes in and out. And it had not been what she had expected.

In the first place, the man had died for hours. She had never heard of this. She had thought of death as coming quickly—a glance of farewell, closing eyes, and—rest. But for hours and hours the struggle had gone on, a fight for breath that all the ward could hear. And he had not closed his eyes at all. They were turned up, and staring.

The Probationer had suffered horribly, and at last she had gone behind the screen and folded her hands and closed her eyes, and said very low, "Dear God—please take him quickly."

He had stopped breathing almost immediately. But that may have been a coincidence.

However, she was not writing that home. Between gasps she was telling the humors of visiting day in the ward, and of how kind every one was to her, which, if not entirely true, was not entirely untrue. They were kind enough when they had time to be, or when they remembered her. Only they did not always remember her.

She ended by saying that she was quite sure they meant to accept her when her three months was up. It was frightfully necessary that she be accepted.

She sent messages to all the little town, which had seen her off almost en masse. And she added that the probationers received the regular first-year allowance of eight dollars a month, and she could make it do nicely—which was quite true, unless she kept on breaking thermometers when she shook them down.

At the end, she sent her love to everybody, including even worthless Johnny Fraser, who cut the grass and scrubbed the porches; and, of course, to Doctor Willie. He was called Doctor Willie because his father, who had taken him into partnership long ago, was Doctor Will. It never had seemed odd, although Doctor Willie was now sixty-five, and a saintly soul.

Curiously enough, her letter was dated April first. Under that very date, and about that time of the day, a health officer in a nearby borough was making an entry regarding certain gentlemen shipped north from Louisiana to work on a railroad. Opposite the name of one Augustus Baird he put a cross. This indicated that Augustus Baird had not been vaccinated.

By the sixth of April, Twenty-two had progressed from splints to a plaster cast and was being most awfully bored. Jane Brown had not returned, and there was a sort of relentless maturity about the nurses who looked after him that annoyed him.

Lying there, he had a good deal of time to study them, and somehow his recollection of the girl with the hunting-case watch did not seem to fit her in with these kindly and efficient women. He could not, for instance, imagine her patronizing the Senior Surgical Intern in a deferential but unmistakable manner, or good-naturedly bullying the First Assistant, who was a nervous person in shoes too small for her, as to their days off duty.

Twenty-two began to learn things about the hospital. For instance, the day nurse, while changing his pillow slips, would observe that Nineteen was going to be operated on that day and close her lips over further information. But when the afternoon relief, while giving him his toothbrush after lunch, said there was a most interesting gallstone case in nineteen, and the night nurse, in reply to a direct question, told Nineteen's name, but nothing else, Twenty-two had a fair working knowledge of the day's events.

He seemed to learn about everything but Jane Brown. He knew when a new baby came, and was even given a glimpse of one, showing, he considered, about the color and general contour of a maraschino cherry. And he learned soon that the god of the hospital is the Staff, although worship did not blind the nurses to their weaknesses.

Thus, the older men, who had been trained before the day of asepsis and modern methods, were revered but carefully watched. They would get out of scrubbing their hands whenever they could, and they hated their beards tied up with gauze. The nurses, keen, competent, and kindly, but shrewd, too, looked after these elderly recalcitrants; loved a few, hated some, and presented to the world unbroken ranks for their defense.

Twenty-two learned also the story of the First Assistant, who was in love with one of the Staff, who was married, and did not care for her anyhow. So she wore tight shoes, and was always beautifully waved, and read Browning.

She had a way of coming in and saying brightly, as if to reassure herself:

"Good morning, Twenty-two. Well, God is still in His heaven, and all's well with the world."

Twenty-two got to feeling awfully uncomfortable about her. She used to bring him flowers and sit down a moment to rest her feet, which generally stung. And she would stop in the middle of a sentence and look into space, but always with a determined smile.

He felt awfully uncomfortable. She was so neat and so efficient—and so tragic. He tried to imagine being hopelessly in love, and trying to live on husks of Browning. Not even Mrs. Browning.

The mind is a curious thing. Suddenly, from thinking of Mrs. Browning, he thought of N. Jane Brown. Of course, not by that ridiculous name. He had learned that she was stationed on that floor. And in the same flash he saw the Senior Surgical Intern swanking about in white ducks and just the object for a probationer to fall in love with. He lay there, and pulled the beginning of the new moustache, and reflected. The First Assistant was pinning a spray of hyacinth in her cap.

"Look here," he said. "Why can't I be put in a wheelchair and get about? One that I can manipulate myself," he added craftily.

She demurred. Indeed, everybody demurred when he put it up to them. But he had gone through the world to the age of twenty-four, getting his own way about ninety-seven per cent of the time. He got it this time, consisting of a new cast, which he named Elizabeth, and a wheelchair, and he spent a full day learning how to steer himself around.

Then, on the afternoon of the third day, rolling back toward the elevator and the *terra incognita* which lay beyond, he saw a sign. He stared at it blankly, because it interfered considerably with a plan he had in mind. The sign was of tin, and it said: "No private patients allowed beyond here."

Twenty-two sat in his chair and stared at it. The plaster cast stretched out in front of him and was covered by a grey blanket. With the exception of the trifling formality of trousers, he was well dressed in a sack coat, a shirt, waistcoat, and a sort of college-boy collar and tie, which one of the orderlies had purchased for him. His other things were in that extremely expensive English car which the city was storing.

The plain truth is that Twenty-two was looking for Jane Brown. Since she had not come to him, he must go to her. He particularly wanted to set her right as to Mabel. And he felt, too, that that trick about respirations had not been entirely fair.

He was, of course, not in the slightest degree in love with her. He had only seen her once, and then he had had a broken leg and a quarter grain of morphine and a burned moustache and no eyebrows left to speak of.

But there was the sign. It was hung to a nail beside the elevator shaft. And far beyond, down the corridor, was somebody in a blue dress and no cap. It might be anybody, but again—

Twenty-two looked around. The elevator had just gone down at its usual rate of a mile every two hours. In the convalescent parlor, where private patients *en negligée* complained about the hospital food, the nurse in charge was making a new cap. Overall, the hospital brooded an after-luncheon peace.

Twenty-two wheeled up under the sign and considered his average of ninety-seven per cent. Followed in sequence these events: (a) Twenty-two wheeled back to the parlor, where old Mr. Simond's cane leaned against a table, and, while engaging that gentleman in conversation, possessed himself of the cane. (b) Wheeled back to the elevator. (c) Drew cane from beneath blanket. (d) Unhooked sign with cane and concealed both under blanket. (e) Worked his way back along the forbidden territory, past I and J until he came to H ward.

Jane Brown was in H ward.

She was alone, and looking very professional. There is nothing quite so professional as a new nurse. She had, indeed, reached a point where, if she took a pulse three times, she got somewhat similar results. There had been a time when they had run something like this: 56, 80, 120.

Jane Brown was taking pulses. It was a visiting day, and all the beds had fresh white spreads, tucked in neatly at the foot. In the exact middle of the center table with its red cloth, was a vase of yellow tulips. The sun came in and turned them to golden flame.

Jane Brown was on duty alone and taking pulses with one eye while she watched the visitors with the other. She did the watching better than she did the pulses. For instance, she was distinctly aware that Stanislas Krzykolski's wife, in the bed next the end, had just slid a half-dozen greasy cakes, sprinkled with sugar, under his pillow. She knew, however, that not only grease but love was in those cakes, and she did not intend to confiscate them until after Mrs. Krzykolski had gone.

More visitors came. Shuffling and self-conscious mill workers, walking on their toes; draggled women; a Chinese boy; a girl with a rouged face and a too confident manner. A hum of conversation hung over the long room. The sunlight came in and turned to glory, not only the tulips and the red tablecloth, but also the brass basins, the fireplace fender, and the Probationer's hair.

Twenty-two sat unnoticed in the doorway. A young girl, very lame, with a mandolin, had just entered the ward. In the little stir of her arrival, Twenty-two had time to see that Jane Brown was worth even all the trouble he had taken, and more.

Really, to see Jane Brown properly, she should have always been seen in the sun. She was that sort.

The lame girl sat down in the center of the ward, and the buzz died away. She was not pretty, and she was very nervous. Twenty-two frowned a trifle.

"Poor devils," he said to himself. But Jane Brown put away her hunting-case watch, and the lame girl swept the ward with soft eyes that had in them a pity that was almost a benediction.

Then she sang. Her voice was like her eyes, very sweet and rather frightened, but tender. And suddenly, something a little hard and selfish in Twenty-two began to be horribly ashamed of itself. And, for no earthly reason in the world, he began to feel like a cumberer of the earth. Before she had finished the first song, he was thinking that perhaps when he was getting about again, he might run over to France for a few months in the ambulance service. A fellow really ought to do his bit.

At just about that point Jane Brown turned and saw him. And although he had run all these risks to get to her, and even then had an extremely cold tin sign lying on his knee under the blanket, at first she did not know him. The shock of this was almost too much for him. In all sorts of places people were glad to see him, especially women. He was astonished, but it was good for him.

She recognized him almost immediately, however, and flushed a little, because she knew he had no business there. She was awfully bound up with rules.

"I came back on purpose to see you," said Twenty-two, when at last the lame girl had limped away. "Because, that day I came in and you looked after me, you know, I—must have talked a lot of nonsense."

"Morphine makes some people talk," she said. It was said in an exact copy of the ward nurse's voice, a frightfully professional and impersonal tone.

"But," said Twenty-two, stirring uneasily, "I said a lot that wasn't true. You may have forgotten, but I haven't. Now that about a girl named Mabel, for instance—"

He stirred again, because, after all, what did it matter what he had said? She was gazing over the ward. She was not interested in him. She had almost forgotten him. And as he stirred Mr. Simond's cane fell out. It was immediately followed by the tin sign, which only gradually subsided, face up, on the bare floor, in a slowly diminishing series of crashes.

Jane Brown stooped and picked them both up and placed them on his lap. Then, very stern, she marched out of the ward into the corridor, and there subsided into quiet hysterics of mirth. Twenty-two, who hated to be laughed at, followed her in the chair, looking extremely annoyed.

"What else was I to do?" he demanded, after a time. "Of course, if you report it, I'm gone."

"What do you intend to do with it now?" she asked. All her professional manner had gone, and she looked alarmingly young.

"If I put it back, I'll only have to steal it again. Because I am absolutely bored to death in that room of mine. I have played a thousand games of solitaire."

The Probationer looked around. There was no one in sight.

"I should think," she suggested, "that if you slipped it behind that radiator, no one would ever know about it."

Fortunately, the ambulance gong set up a clamor below the window just then, and no one heard one of the hospital's most cherished rules going, as one may say, into the discard.

The Probationer leaned her nose against the window and looked down. A colored man was being carried in on a stretcher. Although she did not know it—indeed, never did know it—the gentleman in question was one Augustus Baird.

Soon afterward Twenty-two squeaked—his chair needed oiling—squeaked back to his lonely room and took stock. He found that he was rid of Mabel, but was still a reporter, hurt in doing his duty. He had let this go because he saw that duty was a sort of fetish with the Probationer. And since just now she liked him for what she thought he was, why not wait to tell her until she liked him for himself?

He hoped she was going to like him, because she was going to see him a lot. Also, he liked her even better than he had remembered that he did. She had a sort of thoroughbred look that he liked. And he liked the way her hair was soft and straight and shiny. And he liked the way she was all business and no nonsense. And the way she counted pulses, with her lips moving and a little frown between her eyebrows. And he liked her for being herself—which is, after all, the reason why most men like the women they like, and extremely reasonable.

The First Assistant loaned him Browning that afternoon, and he read *Pippa Passes*. He thought Pippa must have looked like the Probationer.

The Head was a bit querulous that evening. The Heads of Training Schools get that way now and then, although they generally reveal it only to the First Assistant. They have to do so many irreconcilable things, such as keeping down expenses while keeping up requisitions, and remembering the different sorts of sutures the Staff likes, and receiving the Ladies' Committee, and conducting prayers and lectures, and knowing by a swift survey of a ward that the stands have been carbolized and all the toenails cut. Because it is amazing the way toenails grow in bed.

The Head would probably never have come out flatly, but she had a wretched cold, and the First Assistant was giving her a mustard footbath, which was very hot. The Head sat up with a blanket over her shoulders, and read lists while her feet took on the blush of ripe apples. And at last she said, "How is that Probationer with the ridiculous name getting along?"

The First Assistant poured in more hot water.

"N. Jane?" she asked. "Well, she's a nice little thing, and she seems willing. But, of course—"

The Head groaned.

"Nineteen!" she said. "And no character at all. I detest fluttery people. She flutters the moment I go into the ward."

The First Assistant sat back and felt of her cap, which was of starched tulle and was softening a bit from the steam. She felt a thrill of pity for the Probationer. She, too, had once felt fluttery when the Head came in.

"She is very anxious to stay," she observed. "She works hard, too. I—"

"She has no personality, no decision," said the Head, and sneezed twice. She was really very wretched, and so she was unfair. "She is pretty and sweet. But I cannot run my training school on prettiness and sweetness. Has Doctor Harvard come in yet?"

"I—I think not," said the First Assistant. She looked up quickly, but the Head was squeezing a lemon in a cup of hot water beside her.

Now, while the Head was having a footbath, and Twenty-two was having a stock-taking, and Augustus Baird was having his symptoms recorded, Jane Brown was having a shock.

She heard an unmistakable shuffling of feet in the corridor.

Sounds take on much significance in a hospital, and probationers study them, especially footsteps. It gives them a moment sometimes to think what to do next.

Interns, for instance, frequently wear rubber soles on their white shoes and have a way of slipping up on one. And the engineer goes on a half run, generally accompanied by the clanking of a tool or two. And the elevator man runs, too, because generally the bell is ringing. And ward patients shuffle about in carpet slippers, and the pharmacy clerk has a brisk young step, inclined to be jaunty.

But it is the Staff which is always unmistakable. It comes along the corridor deliberately, inexorably. It plants its feet firmly and with authority. It moves with the inevitability of fate, with the pride of royalty, with the ease of the best made-to-order boots. The ring of a Staff member's heel on a hospital corridor is the most authoritative sound on earth. He may be the gentlest soul in the world, but he will tread like royalty.

But this was not Staff. Jane Brown knew this sound, and it filled her with terror. It was the scuffling of four pairs of feet, carefully instructed not to keep step. It meant, in other words, a stretcher. But perhaps it was not coming to her. Ah, but it was!

Panic seized Jane Brown. She knew there were certain things to do, but they went out of her mind like a cat out of a cellar window. However, the ward was watching. It had itself, generally speaking, come in feet first. It knew the procedure. So, instructed by low voices from the beds around, Jane Brown feverishly tore the spread off the emergency bed and drew it somewhat apart from its fellows. Then she stood back and waited.

Came in four officers from the police patrol. Came in the Senior Surgical Intern. Came two convalescents from the next ward to stare in at the door. Came the stretcher, containing a quiet figure under a grey blanket.

Twenty-two, at that exact moment, was putting a queen on a ten spot and pretending there is nothing wrong about cheating oneself.

In a very short time the quiet figure was on the bed, and the Senior Surgical Intern was writing in the order book: "Prepare for operation."

Jane Brown read it over his shoulder, which is not etiquette.

"But—I can't," she quavered. "I don't know how. I won't touch him. He's—he's bloody!"

Then she took another look at the bed and she saw—Johnny Fraser.

Now Johnny had, in his small way, played a part in the Probationer's life, such as occasionally scrubbing porches or borrowing a half dollar or being suspected of stealing the eggs from the henhouse. But *that* Johnny Fraser had been a wicked, smiling imp, much given to sitting in the sun.

Here lay another Johnny Fraser, a quiet one, who might never again feel the warm earth through his worthless clothes on his worthless young body. A Johnny of closed eyes and slow, noisy breathing.

"Why, Johnny!" said the Probationer, in a strangled voice.

The Senior Surgical Intern was interested.

"Know him?" he said.

"He is a boy from home." She was still staring at this quiet, un-impudent figure.

The Senior Surgical Intern eyed her with an eye that was only partially professional. Then he went to the medicine closet and poured a bit of aromatic ammonia into a glass.

"Sit down and drink this," he said, in a very masculine voice. He liked to feel that he could do something for her. Indeed, there was something almost proprietary in the way he took her pulse.

Sometime after the early hospital supper that evening, Twenty-two, having oiled his chair with some olive oil from his tray, made a clandestine trip through the twilight of the corridor back of the elevator shaft. To avoid scandal he pretended interest in other wards, but he gravitated, as a needle to the pole, to H. And there he found the Probationer, looking rather strained, and mothering a quiet figure on a bed.

He was a trifle puzzled at her distress, for she made no secret of Johnny's status in the community.

What he did not grasp was that Johnny Fraser was a link between this new and rather terrible world of the hospital and home. It was not Johnny alone, it was Johnny scrubbing a home porch and doing it badly, it was Johnny in her father's old clothes, it was Johnny fishing for catfish in the creek, or lending his pole to one of the little brothers whose pictures were on her table in the dormitory.

Twenty-two felt a certain depression. He reflected rather grimly that he had been ten days missing and that no one had apparently given a hang whether he turned up or not.

"Is he going to live?" he inquired. He could see that the ward nurse had an eye on him, and was preparing for retreat.

"O yes," said Jane Brown. "I think so now. The Intern says they have had a message from Doctor Willie. He is coming." There was a beautiful confidence in her tone.

Things moved very fast with the Probationer for the next twenty-four hours. Doctor Willie came, looking weary but smiling benevolently. Jane Brown met him in a corridor and kissed him, as, indeed, she had been in the habit of doing since her babyhood.

"Where is the young rascal?" said Doctor Willie. "Up to his old tricks, Nellie, and struck by a train."

He put a hand under her chin, which is never done to the members of the training school in a hospital, and searched her face with his kind old eyes. "Well, how does it go, Nellie?"

Jane Brown swallowed hard.

"All right," she managed. "They want to operate, Doctor Willie."

"Tut!" he said. "Always in a hurry, these hospitals. We'll wait a while, I think. Is everybody well at home?"

It had come to her, you see, what comes to every nurse once in her training—the thinness of the veil, the terror of calamity, the fear of death.

"All well. And—" he glanced around. Only the Senior Surgical Intern was in sight, and he was out of hearing. "Look here, Nellie," he said, "I've got a dozen fresh eggs for you in my satchel. Your mother sent them."

She nearly lost her professional manner again then. But she only asked him to warn the boys about automobiles and riding on the backs of wagons.

Had any one said Twenty-two to her, she would not have known what was meant. Not just then, anyhow.

In the doctors' room that night the Senior Surgical Intern lighted a cigarette and telephoned to the operating room.

"That trephining's off," he said, briefly.

Then he fell to conversation with the Senior Medical, who was rather worried about a case listed on the books as Augustus Baird.

Twenty-two did not sleep very well that night. He needed exercise, he felt. But there was something else. Miss Brown had been just a shade too ready to accept his explanation about Mabel, he felt, so ready that he feared she had been more polite than sincere. Probably she still believed there was a Mabel. Not that it mattered, except that he hated to make a fool of himself. He roused once in the night and was quite sure he heard her voice down the corridor. He knew this must be wrong, because they would not make her work all day and all night, too.

But, as it happened, it *was* Jane Brown. The hospital provided plenty of sleeping time, but now and then there was a slip-up and somebody paid. There had been a night operation, following on a busy day, and the operating room nurses needed help. Out of a sound sleep, the night Assistant had summoned Jane Brown to clean instruments.

At five o'clock that morning, she was still sitting on a stool beside a glass table, polishing instruments which made her shiver. All around were things that were spattered with blood. But she looked anything but fluttery. She was a very grim and determined young person just then, and professional beyond belief. The other things, like washing windowsills and cutting toenails, had had no significance. But here she was at last on the edge of mercy. Someone who might have died had lived that night because of this room, and these instruments, and willing hands.

She hoped she would always have willing hands.

She looked very pale at breakfast the next morning, and rather older. Also, she had a new note of authority in her voice when she telephoned the kitchen and demanded H ward's soft-boiled eggs. She washed windowsills that morning again, but no longer was there rebellion in her soul. She was seeing suddenly how the hospital required all these menial services, which were not menial at all but only preparation; that there were little tasks and big ones, and one graduated from the one to the other.

She took some flowers from the ward bouquet and put them beside Johnny's bed—Johnny, who was still lying quiet, with closed eyes.

The Senior Surgical Intern did a dressing in the ward that morning. He had been in to see Augustus Baird, and he felt uneasy. He vented it on Tony, who had a stiletto thrust in his neck, by jerking at the adhesive. Tony wailed, and Jane Brown, who was the "dirty" nurse—which does not mean what it appears to mean, but is the person who receives the soiled dressings—Jane Brown gritted her teeth.

"Keep quiet," said the S.S.I., who was a good fellow, but had never been stabbed in the neck for running away with somebody else's wife.

"It hurts!" said Tony with his Italian accent.

Jane Brown turned very pink.

"Why don't you let me cut it off properly?" she said, in a strangled tone.

The total result of this was that Jane Brown was reprimanded by the First Assistant, and learned some things about ethics.

"But," she protested, "it was both stupid and cruel. And if I know I am right—"

"How are you to know you are right?" demanded the First Assistant, crossly. Her feet were stinging. "'A little knowledge is a dangerous thing.'" This was a favorite quotation of hers, although not Browning. "Nurses in hospitals are there to carry out the doctor's orders. Not to think or to say what they think unless they are asked. To be intelligent, but—"

"But not too intelligent!" said the Probationer. "I see."

This was duly reported to the Head, who observed that it was merely what she had expected and extremely pert. Her cold was hardly any better.

It was taking the Probationer quite a time to realize her own total lack of significance in all this. She had been accustomed to men who rose when a woman entered a room and remained standing as long as she stood. And now she was in a new world, where she had to rise and remain standing while a cocky youth in ducks, just out of medical college, sauntered in with his hands in his pockets and took a boutonnière from the ward bouquet.

It was probably extremely good for her.

She was frightfully tired that day, and toward evening the little glow of service began to fade. There seemed to be nothing to do for Johnny but to wait. Doctor Willie had seemed to think that nature would clear matters up there, and had requested no operation. She smoothed beds and carried cups of water and broke another thermometer. And she put the eggs from home in the ward pantry and made eggnog of them for Stanislas Krzykolski, who was unaccountably upset as to stomach.

She had entirely forgotten Twenty-two. He had stayed away all that day, in a sort of faint hope that she would miss him. But she had not. She was feeling rather worried, to tell the truth. For a Staff surgeon going through the ward, had stopped by Johnny's bed and examined the pupils of his eyes, and had then exchanged a glance with the Senior Surgical Intern that had perplexed her.

In the chapel at prayers that evening all around her the nurses sat and rested, their tired hands folded in their laps. They talked a little among themselves, but it was only a buzzing that reached the Probationer faintly. Someone near was talking about something that was missing.

"Gone?" she said. "Of course it is gone. The bathroom man reported it to me and I went and looked."

"But who in the world would take it?"

"My dear," said the first speaker, "who *does* take things in a hospital, anyhow? Only—a tin sign!"

It was then that the Head came in. She swept in; her grey gown, her grey hair gave her a majesty that filled the Probationer with awe. Behind her came the First Assistant with the prayer book and hymnal. The Head believed in form.

Jane Brown offered up a little prayer that night for Johnny Fraser, and another little one without words, that Doctor Willie was right. She sat and rested her weary young body, and remembered how

Doctor Willie was loved and respected, and the years he had cared for the whole countryside. And the peace of the quiet room, with the Easter lilies on the tiny altar, brought rest to her.

It was when prayers were over that the Head made her announcement. She rose and looked over the shadowy room, where among the rows of white caps only the Probationer's head was uncovered, and she said:

"I have an announcement to make to the training school. One which I regret, and which will mean a certain amount of hardship and deprivation.

"A case of contagion has been discovered in one of the wards, and it has been considered necessary to quarantine the hospital. The doors were closed at seven-thirty this evening."

II

Considering that he could not get out anyhow, Twenty-two took the news of the quarantine calmly. He reflected that, if he was shut in, Jane Brown was shut in also. He had a wicked hope, at the beginning, that the Senior Surgical Intern had been shut out, but at nine o'clock that evening, that young gentleman showed up at the door of his room, said "Cheerio," came in, helped himself to a cigarette, gave a professional glance at Twenty-two's toes, which were all that was un-plastered of the leg, and departing, threw back over his shoulder his sole conversational effort:

"Hell of a mess, isn't it?"

Twenty-two took up again gloomily the book he was reading, *Diseases of the Horse,* from the hospital library. He was in the midst of Glanders.

He had, during most of that day, been making up his mind to let his family know where he was. He did not think they cared, particularly. He had no illusions about that. But there was something about Jane Brown which made him feel like doing the decent thing. It annoyed him frightfully, but there it was. She was so eminently the sort of person who believed in doing the decent thing.

So, about seven o'clock, he had sent the orderly out for stamps and paper. He imagined that Jane Brown would not think writing home on hospital stationery a good way to break bad news. But the orderly had stopped for a chat at the engine house, and had ended by playing a game of dominoes. When, at ten o'clock, he had returned to the hospital entrance, the richer by a quarter and a glass of beer, he had found a strange policeman on the hospital steps, and the doors locked.

The quarantine was on.

Now there are different sorts of quarantines. There is the sort where a trained nurse and the patient are shut up in a room and bath, and the family only opens the door and peers in. And there is the sort where the front door has a placard on it, and the family goes in and out the back way, and takes a streetcar to the office, the same as usual. And there is the hospital quarantine, which is the real thing, because hospitals are expected to do things thoroughly.

So our hospital was closed up as tight as a jar of preserves. There were policemen at all the doors, quite suddenly. They locked the doors and put the keys in their pockets, and from that time on, they opened them only to pass things in, such as newspapers or milk or groceries or the braver members of the Staff. But not to let anything out—except the Staff. Supposedly Staffs do not carry germs.

And, indeed, even the Staff was not keen about entering. It thought of a lot of things it ought to do about visiting time, and prescribed considerably over the telephone.

At first there was a great deal of confusion, because quite a number of people had been out on various errands when it happened. And they came back, and protested to the office that they had only their uniforms on under their coats, and three dollars; or their slippers and no hats. Or that they would sue the city. One or two of them got quite desperate and tried to crawl up the fire escape, but failed.

This is of interest chiefly because it profoundly affected Jane Brown. Miss McAdoo, her ward nurse, had debated whether to wash her hair that evening or to take a walk. She had decided on the walk and was therefore shut out, along with the Junior Medical, the kitchen cat, the Superintendent's mother-in-law and six other nurses.

The next morning the First Assistant gave Jane Brown charge of H ward.

"It's very irregular," she said. "I don't exactly know—you have only one bad case, haven't you?"

"Only Johnny."

The First Assistant absent-mindedly ran a finger over the top of a table, and examined it for dust.

"Of course," she said, "it's a great chance for you. Show that you can handle this ward, and you are practically safe."

Jane Brown drew a long breath and stood up very straight. Then she ran her eye over the ward. There was something vaguely reminiscent of Miss McAdoo in her glance.

Twenty-two made three brief excursions back along the corridor that first day of the quarantine. But Jane Brown was extremely professional and very busy. There was an air of discipline over the ward. Let a man but so much as turn over in bed and show an inch of blanket, and she pounced on the bed and reduced it to the most horrible neatness. All the beds looked as if they had been made up with a carpenter's square.

On the third trip, however, Jane Brown was writing at the table. Twenty-two wheeled himself into the doorway and eyed her with disapproval.

"What do you mean by sitting down?" he demanded sarcastically. "Don't you know that now you are in charge you ought to keep moving?"

To which she replied, absently, "Three buttered toasts, two dry toasts, six soft boiled eggs, and twelve soups." She was working on the diet slips.

Then she smiled at him. They were quite old friends already. It is curious about love and friendship and all those kindred emotions. They do not grow nearly so fast when people are together as when they are apart. It is an actual fact that the growth of many an intimacy is checked by meetings. Because when people are apart, it is what they *are* that counts, and when they are together it is what they do and say and look like. Many a beautiful affair has been ruined because, just as it was going along well, the principals met again.

However, all this merely means that Twenty-two and Jane Brown were infinitely closer friends than four or five meetings would really indicate.

The ward was very quiet on this late afternoon call of his save for Johnny's heavy breathing. There is a quiet hour in a hospital, between afternoon temperatures and the ringing of the bell which means that the suppers for the wards are on their way—a quiet hour when over the long rows of beds broods the peace of the ending day.

It is a melancholy hour, too, because from the streets comes faintly the echo of feet hurrying home, the eager trot of a horse bound stableward. To those in the eddy that is the ward comes at this time a certain heaviness of spirit. Poor thing though home may have been, they long for it.

In H ward that late afternoon, there was a wave of homesickness in the air, and on the part of those men who were up and about, who shuffled up and down the ward in flapping carpet slippers, an inclination to mutiny.

"How did they take it?" Twenty-two inquired. She puckered her eyebrows.

"They don't like it," she confessed. "Some of them were about ready to go home and it—*Tony!*" she called sharply.

For Tony, who had been cunningly standing by the window leading to a fire escape, had flung the window up and was giving unmistakable signs of climbing out and returning to the other man's wife.

"Tony!" she called, and ran. Tony scrambled up on the sill. A sort of titter ran over the ward and Tony, now on the platform outside, waved a derisive hand through the window.

"Goodbye, miss!" he said, and disappeared.

It was not a very dramatic thing, after all. It is chiefly significant for its effect on Twenty-two, who was obliged to sit frozen with horror and cursing his broken leg, while Jane Brown raced Tony down the fire escape and caught him at the foot of it. Tony took a look around. The courtyard gates were closed, and a policeman sat outside on a camp stool reading the newspaper. Tony smiled sheepishly and surrendered.

Some seconds later, Tony and Jane Brown appeared on the platform outside. Jane Brown had Tony by the ear, and she stopped long enough outside to exchange the ear for his shoulder, by which she shook him, vigorously.

Twenty-two turned his chair around and wheeled himself back to his room. He was filled with a cold rage—because she might have fallen on the fire escape and been killed; because he had not been able to help her; because she was there, looking after the

derelicts of life, when the world was beautiful outside, and she was young; because to her he was just
Twenty-two and nothing more.

He had seen her exactly six times.

Jane Brown gave the ward a little talk that night before the night nurse reported. She stood in the center
of the long room, beside the tulips, and said that she
was going to be alone there, and that she would have to
put the situation up to their sense of honor. If they
tried to escape, they would hurt her. Also they would
surely be caught and brought back. And, because she
believed in a combination of faith and deeds, she took
three nails and the linen room flatiron, and nailed shut
the window onto the fire escape.

After that, she brushed crumbs out of the beds
with a whiskbroom, and rubbed a few backs with
alcohol, and smoothed the counterpanes, and hung
over Johnny's unconscious figure for a little while,
giving motherly pats to his flat pillow and worrying
considerably because there was so little about him to
remind her of the Johnny she knew at home.

After that, she sat down and made up her records for the night nurse. The ward understood and
was perfectly good, trying hard not to muss its pil-
lows or wrinkle the covers. And struggling, too, with
a new idea. They were prisoners. No more release

cards would brighten the days. For an indefinite period, the old Frenchman would moan at night, and Bader, the German, would snore, and the Chinese fellow would cough. Indefinitely, they would eat soft-boiled eggs and rice and beef tea and cornstarch.

The ward felt extremely low in its mind.

That night, the Senior Surgical Intern went in to play cribbage with Twenty-two, and received a lecture on leaving a young girl alone in H with a lot of desperate men. They both grew rather heated over the discussion and forgot to play cribbage at all. Twenty-two lay awake half the night, because he had seen clearly that the Senior Surgical Intern was interested in Jane Brown also, and would probably loaf around H most of the time since there would be no new cases now. It was a crowning humiliation to have the night nurse apply to the Senior Surgical Intern for a sleeping powder for him!

Toward morning, he remembered that he had promised to write out from memory one of the *Sonnets from the Portuguese* for the First Assistant, and he turned on the light and jotted down two lines of it. He wrote:

> *For we two look two ways, and cannot shine*
> *With the same sunlight on our brow and hair.*

And then sat up in bed for half an hour looking at it because he was so awfully afraid it was true of Jane Brown and himself. Not, of course, that he wanted to shine at all. It was the looking two ways that hurt.

The next evening, the nurses took their airing on the roof, which was a sooty place with a parapet, and in the courtyard, which was an equally sooty place with a wispy fountain. And because the whole situation was new, they formed in little groups on the wooden benches and sang, hands folded on white aprons, heads lifted, eyes upturned to where, above the dimly lighted windows, the stars peered palely through the smoke.

The S.S.I. sauntered out. He had thought he saw the Probationer from his window, and in the new relaxation of discipline, he saw a chance to join her. But the figure he had thought he recognized proved to be someone else, and he fell to wandering alone up and down the courtyard.

He was trying to work out this problem: would the advantage of marrying early and thus being considered eligible for certain cases, offset the disadvantage of the extra expense?

He decided to marry early and hang the expense.

The days went by, three, then four, and a little line of tension deepened around Jane Brown's mouth. Perhaps it has not been mentioned that she had a fighting nose, short and straight, and a wistful mouth. For Johnny Fraser was still lying in a stupor.

Jane Brown felt that something was wrong. Doctor Willie came in once or twice, making the long trip without complaint and without hope of payment. All his busy life, he had worked for the sake of work, and not for reward. He called her "Nellie," to the delight of the ward, which began to love him, and he spent a long hour each time by Johnny's bed. But the Probationer was quick to realize that the Senior Surgical Intern disapproved of him.

That young man had developed a tendency to wander into H at odd hours and sit on the edge of a table, leaving Jane Brown divided between proper respect for an intern and fury over the wrinkling of her table covers. It was during one of these visits that she spoke of Doctor Willie.

"Because he is a country practitioner," she said, "you—you patronize him."

"Not at all," said the Senior Surgical Intern. "Personally I like him immensely."

"Personally!"

The Senior Surgical Intern waved a hand toward Johnny's bed.

"Look there," he said. "You don't think that chap's getting any better, do you?"

"If," said Jane Brown, with suspicious quiet, "if you think you know more than a man who has practiced for forty years and saved more people than you ever saw, why don't you tell him so?"

There is really no defense for this conversation. Discourse between a probationer and an intern is supposed to be limited to yea, yea, and nay, nay. But the circumstances were unusual.

"Tell him!" exclaimed the Senior Surgical Intern, "and be called before the Executive Committee and fired! Dear girl, I am inexpressibly flattered, but the voice of an intern in a hospital is the voice of one crying in the wilderness."

Twenty-two, who was out on crutches that day for the first time, and was looking very big and extremely awkward, Twenty-two looked back from the elevator shaft and scowled. He seemed always to see a flash of white duck near the door of H ward.

To add to his chagrin, the Senior Surgical Intern clapped him on the back in congratulation a moment later, and nearly upset him. He had intended to go back to the ward and discuss a plan he had, but he was very morose those days and really not a companionable person. He stumped back to his room and resolutely went to bed.

There he lay for a long time looking at the ceiling, and saying, out of his misery, things not necessary to repeat.

So Twenty-two went to bed and sulked, refusing supper, and having the word "Vicious" marked on his record by the nurse, who hoped he would see it sometime. And Jane Brown went and sat beside a strangely silent Johnny and worried. And the Senior Surgical Intern went down to the pharmacy and thereby altered a number of things.

The pharmacy clerk had been shaving—his own bedroom was dark—and he saw the Senior Surgical Intern in the little mirror hung on the window frame.

"Hello," he said, over the soap. "Shut the door."

The Senior Surgical Intern shut the door, and then sniffed. "Smells like a bar-room," he commented.

The pharmacy clerk shaved the left angle of his jaw, and then turned around.

"Little experiment of mine," he explained. "Simple syrup, grain alcohol, a dash of cochineal for coloring, and some flavoring extract. It's an imitation cordial. Try it."

The Senior Surgical Intern was not a drinker, but he was willing to try anything once. So he secured a two-ounce medicine glass, and filled it.

"Looks nice," he commented, and tasted it. "It's not bad."

"Not bad!" said the pharmacy clerk. "You'd pay four dollars a bottle for that stuff in a hotel. Actual cost here, about forty cents."

The Senior Surgical Intern sat down and stretched out his legs. He had the glass in his hand.

"It's rather sweet," he said. "But it looks pretty." He took another sip.

After he had finished it, he got to thinking things over. He felt about seven feet tall and very important, and not at all like a voice crying in the wilderness. He had a strong inclination to go into the Superintendent's office and tell him where he went wrong in running the institution—which he re-strained. And another to go up to H and tell Jane Brown the truth about Johnny Fraser—which he yielded to.

On the way up he gave the elevator man a cigar.

He was very explicit with Jane Brown.

"Your man's wrong, that's all there is about it," he said. "I can't say anything, and you can't. But he's wrong. That's an operative case. The Staff knows it."

"Then, why doesn't the Staff do it?"

The Senior Surgical Intern was still feeling very tall. He looked down at her from a great distance.

"Because, dear child," he said, "it's your man's case. You ought to know enough about professional ethics for that."

He went away, then, and had a violent headache, which he blamed on confinement and lack of exercise. But he had sowed something in the Probationer's mind.

For she knew, suddenly, that he had been right. The Staff had meant that, then, when they looked at Johnny and shook their heads. The Staff knew, the hospital knew. Every one knew but Doctor Willie. But Doctor Willie had the case. Back in her little town, Johnny's mother was looking to Doctor Willie, believing in him, hoping through him.

That night, Twenty-two slept, and Jane Brown lay awake. And down in H ward, Johnny Fraser had a bad spell at that hour toward dawn when the vitality is low, and men die. He did not die, however. But the night nurse recorded, "Pulse very thin and iregular," at four o'clock.

She, too, was not a famous speller.

During the next morning, while the ward rolled bandages, having carefully scrubbed its hands first,

Jane Brown wrote records—she did it rather well now—and then arranged the pins in the ward pin-cushion. She made concentric circles of safety-pins outside and common pins inside, with a large H in the center. But her mind was not on this artistic bit of creation. It was on Johnny Fraser.

She made up her mind to speak to Doctor Willie.

Twenty-two had got over his sulking or his jealousy, or whatever it was, and during the early hours, those hours when Johnny was hardly breathing, he had planned something. He thought that he did it to interest the patients and make them contented, but somewhere in the back of his mind he knew it was to see more of Jane Brown. He planned a concert in the chapel.

So that morning, he took Elizabeth, the plaster cast, back to H ward, where Jane Brown was fixing the pincushion, and had a good minute of feasting his eyes on her while she was sucking a jabbed finger. She knew she should have dipped the finger in a solution, but habit is strong in most of us.

Twenty-two had a wild desire to offer to kiss the finger and make it well. This, however, was not habit. It was insanity. He recognized this himself, and felt more than a trifle worried about it, because he had been in love quite a number of times before, but he had never had this sort of feeling.

He put the concert up to her with a certain amount of anxiety. If she could sing, or play, or recite—although he hoped she would not recite—all would be well. But if she refused to take any part, he did not intend to have a concert. That was flat.

"I can play," she said, making a neat period after the H on the pincushion.

He was awfully relieved.

"Good," he said. "You know, I like the way you say that. It's so—well, it's so competent." He got out a notebook and wrote "Miss Brown, piano selections."

It was while he was writing that Jane Brown had a sort of mental picture—the shabby piano at home, kicked below by many childish feet, but mellow and sweet, like an old violin, and herself sitting practicing, over and over, that part of Paderewski's Minuet where, as every one knows, the fingering is rather difficult, and outside the open window, leaning on his broom, worthless Johnny Fraser, staring in with friendly eyes and an extremely dirty face. To Twenty-two's unbounded amazement, she flung down the cushion and made for the little ward linen room.

He found her there a moment later, her arms outstretched on the table and her face buried in them. Someone had been boiling a rubber tube and had let the pan go dry. Ever afterward, Twenty-two was to associate the smell of burning rubber with Jane Brown, and with his first real knowledge that he was in love with her.

He stumped in after her and closed the door, and might have ruined everything then and there by taking her in his arms, crutch and all. But the smell of burning rubber is a singularly permeating one, and he was kept from one indiscretion by being discovered in another.

It was somewhat later that Jane Brown was reprimanded for being found in the linen room with a private patient. She made no excuse, but something a little defiant began to grow in her eyes. It was not that she loved her work less. She was learning, day by day, the endless sacrifices of this profession she had chosen, its unselfishness, its grinding hard work, the payment that may lie in a smile of gratitude, the agony of pain that cannot be relieved.

She went through her days with hands held out for service, and at night, in the chapel, she whispered soundless little prayers to be accepted, and to be always gentle and kind. She did not want to become a machine. She knew, although she had no words for it, the difference between duty and service.

But—a little spirit of rebellion was growing in her breast. She did not understand about Johnny Fraser, for one thing. And the matter of the linen room hurt. There seemed to be too many rules.

Then, too, she began to learn that hospitals had limitations. Jane Brown's hospital had no social worker. Much as she loved the work, the part that the hospital could not do began to hurt her. Before the quarantine women with new babies had gone out, without an idea of where to spend the night. Ailing children had gone home to such places as she could see from the dormitory windows, where the work the hospital had begun could not be finished.

From the roof of the building at night she looked out over a city that terrified her. The call of a playing child in the street began to sound to her like the shriek of accident. The very grinding of the trolley cars, the smoke of the mills, began to mean the operating room. She thought a great deal, those days, about the little town she had come from, with its peace and quiet streets. The city seemed cruel. But now and then she learned that if cities are cruel, men are kind.

Thus, on the very day of the concert, the quarantine was broken for a few minutes. It was broken forcibly, and by an officer of the law. A little newsie, standing by a fire at the next corner, for the spring day was cold, had caught fire. The big corner man had seen it all. He stripped off his overcoat, rolled the boy in it, and ran to the hospital. Here he was confronted by a brother officer, who was forbidden to admit him. The corner man did the thing that seemed quickest. He laid the newsie on the ground, knocked out the quarantine officer in two blows, broke the glass of the door with a third, slipped a bolt, and then, his burden in his arms, stalked in.

It did not lessen the majesty of that entrance that he was crying all the time.

The Probationer pondered that story when she heard it. After all, laws were right and good, but there were higher things than laws. She went and stood by Johnny's bed for a long time, thinking.

In the meantime, unexpected talent for the concert had developed. The piano in the chapel proving out of order, the elevator man proved to have been a piano tuner. He tuned it with a bone forceps. Strange places, hospitals, into which drift men from every walk of life, to find a haven and peace within their quiet walls. Old Tony had sung, in his youth, in the opera at Milan.

A pretty young nurse went around the corridors muttering bits of *Little Orphant Annie* to herself. The

Senior Surgical Intern was to sing the "Rosary," and went about practicing to himself. He came into H ward and sang it through for Jane Brown, with his heart in his clear young eyes. He sang about the hours he had spent with her being strings of pearls, and all that, but he was really asking her if she would be willing to begin life with him in a little house, where she would have to answer the doorbell and watch telephone calls while he was out.

Jane Brown felt something of this, too. For she said, "You sing it beautifully," although he had flatted at least three times.

He wrote his name on a medicine label and glued it to her hand. It looked alarmingly possessive.

Twenty-two presided at the concert that night. He was extravagantly funny, and the sort of creaking solemnity with which things began turned to up-roarious laughter very soon.

Everything went off wonderfully. Tony started his selection too high, and was obliged to stop and begin over again. And the two Silversteins, from the children's ward, who were to dance a Highland fling together, had a violent quarrel at the last moment and had to be scratched. But everything else went well. The ambulance driver gave a bass solo, and kept a bar or two ahead of the accompaniment, dodging chords as he did wagons on the street, and fetching up with a sort of garrison finish much as he brought in the ambulance.

But the real musical event of the evening was Jane Brown's playing. She played Schubert without any notes, because she had been taught to play Schubert that way.

And when they called her back, she played little folk songs of the far places of Europe. Standing around the walls, in wheelchairs, on crutches, pale with the hospital pallor, these aliens in their eddy listened and thrilled. Some of them wept, but they smiled also.

At the end she played the Minuet, with a sort of flaming look in her eyes that puzzled Twenty-two. He could not know that she was playing it to Johnny Fraser, lying with closed eyes in the ward upstairs. He did not realize that there was a passion of sacrifice throbbing behind the dignity of the music.

Doctor Willie had stayed over for the concert. He sat, beaming benevolently, in the front row, and toward the end, he got up and told some stories. After all, it was Doctor Willie who was the real hit of the evening. The convalescents rocked with joy in their roller chairs. Crutches came down in loud applause. When he sat down he slipped a big hand over Jane Brown's and gave hers a hearty squeeze.

"How d'you like me as a parlor entertainer, Nellie?" he whispered.

She put her other hand over his. Somehow she could not speak.

The First Assistant called to the Probationer that night as she went past her door. Lights were out, so the First Assistant had a candle, and she was rubbing her feet with witch hazel.

"Come in," she called. "I have been looking for you. I have some news for you."

The exaltation of the concert had died away. Jane Brown, in the candle light, looked small and tired and very, very young.

"We have watched you carefully," said the First Assistant, who had her night garments on but had forgotten to take off her cap. "Although you are young, you have shown ability, and you are to be accepted."

"Thank you, very much," replied Jane Brown, in a strangled tone.

"At first," said the First Assistant, "we were not sure. You were very young, and you had such odd ideas. You know that yourself now."

She leaned down and pressed a sore little toe with her forefinger. Then she sighed. The mention of Jane Brown's youth had hurt her, because she was no longer very young. And there were times when she was tired, when it seemed to her that only youth counted. She felt that way tonight.

When Jane Brown had gone on, she blew out her candle and went to bed, still in her cap.

Hospitals do not really sleep at night. The elevator man dozes in his cage, and the night watchman may nap in the engineer's room in the basement. But the night nurses are always making their sleepless rounds, and in the wards, dark and quiet, restless figures turn and sigh.

Before she went to bed that night, Jane Brown, by devious ways, slipped back to her ward. It looked strange to her, this cavernous place, filled with the unlovely noises of sleeping men. By the one low light near the doorway, she went back to Johnny's bed, and sat down beside him. She felt that this was the place to think things out. In her room, other things pressed in on her; the necessity of making good for the sake of those at home, her love of the work, and cowardice. But here, she saw things right.

The night nurse found her there sometime later, asleep, her hunting-case watch open on Johnny's bed and her fingers still on his quiet wrist. She made no report of it.

Twenty-two had another sleepless night written in on his record that night. He sat up and worried. He worried about the way the Senior Surgical Intern had sung to Jane Brown that night. And he worried about things he had done and shouldn't have, and things he should have done and hadn't. Mostly the first.

At five in the morning, he wrote a letter to his family telling them where he was and that he had been vaccinated and that the letter would be fumigated. He also wrote a check for an artificial leg for the boy in the children's ward, and then went to bed and put himself to sleep by reciting the rosary over and over. His last conscious thought was that the hours he had spent with a certain person would not make much of a string of pearls.

The Probationer went to Doctor Willie the next day. Some of the exuberance of the concert still bubbled in him, although he shook his head over Johnny's record.

"A little slow, Nellie," he said. "A little slow."

Jane Brown took a long breath.

"Doctor Willie," she said, "won't you have him operated on?"

He looked up at her over his spectacles.

"Operated on? What for?"

"Well, he's not getting any better," she managed desperately. "I'm—sometimes I think he'll die while we're waiting for him to get better."

He was surprised, but he was not angry.

"There's no fracture, child," he said gently. "If there is a clot there, nature is probably better at removing it than we are. The trouble with you," he said indulgently, "is that you have come here, where they operate first and regret afterward. Nature is the best surgeon, child."

She cast about her despairingly for some way to tell him the truth. But even when she spoke, she knew she was foredoomed to failure.

"But suppose the Staff thinks that he should be?"

Doctor Willie's kindly mouth set itself into grim lines.

"The Staff!" he said, and looked at her searchingly. Then his jaws set at an obstinate angle.

"Well, Nellie," he said, "I guess one opinion's as good as another in these cases. And I don't suppose they'll do any cutting and hacking without my consent." He looked at Johnny's unconscious figure. "He never amounted to much," he added, "but it's surprising the way money's been coming in to pay his board here. Your mother sent five dollars. A good lot of people are interested in him. I can't see myself going home and telling them he died on the operating table."

He patted her on the arm as he went out.

"Don't get an old head on those young shoulders yet, Nellie," he said as he was going. "Leave the worrying to me. I'm used to it."

She saw then that to him she was still a little girl. She probably would always be just a little girl to him. He did not take her seriously, and no one else would speak to him. She was quite despairing.

The ward loved Doctor Willie since the night before. It watched him out with affectionate eyes. Jane Brown watched him, too, his fine old head, the sturdy step that had brought healing and peace to a whole county. She had hurt him, she knew that. She ached at the thought of it. And she had done no good.

That afternoon, Jane Brown broke another rule. She went to Twenty-two on her off duty, and caused a mild furor there. He had been drawing a sketch of her from memory, an extremely poor sketch, with one eye larger than the other. He hid it immediately, although she could not possibly have recognized it, and talked very fast to cover his excitement.

"Well, well!" he said. "I knew I was going to have some luck today. My right hand has been itching—or is that a sign of money?" Then he saw her face and reduced his speech to normality, if not his heart.

"Come and sit down," he said. "And tell me about it."

But she would not sit down. She went to the window and looked out for a moment. It was from there she said, "I have been accepted."

"Good." But he did not, apparently, think it such good news. He drew a long breath. "Well, I suppose your friends should be glad for you."

"I didn't come to talk about being accepted," she announced.

"I don't suppose, by any chance, you came to see how I am getting along?" he inquired humbly.

"I can see that."

"You can't see how lonely I am." When she offered nothing to this speech, he enlarged on it. "When it gets unbearable," he said, "I sit in front of the mirror and keep myself company. If that doesn't make your heart ache, nothing will."

"I'm afraid I have heartache, but it is not that." For a terrible moment, he thought of that theory of his which referred to a disappointment in love. Was she going to have the unbelievable cruelty to tell him about it?

"I have to talk to somebody," she said simply. "And I came to you, because you've worked on a newspaper, and you have had a lot of experience. It's a matter of ethics. But really it's a matter of life and death."

He felt most horribly humble before her, and he hated the lie, except that it had brought her to him. There was something so direct and childlike about her. The very way she drew a chair in front of him and proceeded, talking rather fast, to lay the matter before him, touched him profoundly. He felt, somehow, incredibly old and experienced.

And then, after all that, to fail her!

"You see how it is," she finished. "I can't go to the Staff, and they wouldn't do anything if I did— except possibly put me out. Because a nurse really only follows orders. And I've got to stay, if I can. And Doctor Willie doesn't believe in an operation and won't see that he's dying. And everybody at home thinks he is right, because—well," she added hastily, "he's been right a good many times."

He listened attentively. His record, you remember, was his own way some ninety-seven per cent of the time, and at first, he would not believe that this was going to be the three per cent, or a part of it.

"Well," he said at last, "we'll just make the Staff turn in and do it. That's easy."

"But they won't. They can't."

"We can't let Johnny die, either, can we?"

But when at last she was gone, and the room was incredibly empty without her—when, to confess a fact that he was exceedingly shame-faced about, he had wheeled over to the chair she had sat in and put his cheek against the arm where her hand had rested, when he was somewhat his own man again and had got over the feeling that his arms were empty of something they had never held—then it was that Twenty-two found himself up against the three per cent.

The hospital's attitude was firm. It could not interfere. It was an outside patient and an outside doctor. Its responsibility ended with providing for the care of the patient, under his physician's orders. It was regretful—but, of course, unless the case was turned over to the Staff.

He went back to the ward to tell her, after it had all been explained to him. But she was not surprised. He saw that, after all, she had really known he was going to fail her.

"It's hopeless," was all she said. "Everybody is right, and everybody is wrong."

It was the next day that, going to the courtyard for a breath of air, she saw a woman outside the iron gate waving to her. It was Johnny's mother, a forlorn old soul in what Jane Brown recognized as an old suit of her mother's.

"Doctor Willie bought my ticket, Miss Nellie," she said nervously. "It seems like I had to come, even if I couldn't get in. I've been waiting around most all afternoon. How is he?"

"He is resting quietly," said Jane Brown, holding herself very tense, because she wanted to scream. "He isn't suffering at all."

"Could you tell me which window he's near, Miss Nellie?"

She pointed out the window, and Johnny Fraser's mother stood, holding to the bars, peering up at it. Her lips moved, and Jane Brown knew that she was praying. At last she turned her eyes away.

"Folks have said a lot about him," she said, "but he was always a good son to me. If only he'd had a chance—I'd be right worried, Miss Nellie, if he didn't have Doctor Willie looking after him."

Jane Brown went into the building. There was just one thing clear in her mind. Johnny Fraser must have his chance, somehow.

In the meantime, things were not doing any too well in the hospital. A second case, although mild, had extended the quarantine. Discontent grew and threatened to develop into mutiny. Six men from one of the wards marched en masse to the lower hall, and were preparing to rush the guards when they were discovered. The Senior Surgical Intern took two prisoners himself, and became an emergency case for two stitches and arnica compresses.

Jane Brown helped to fix him up, and he took advantage of her holding a dressing basin near his cut lip to kiss her hand, very respectfully. She would have resented it under other circumstances, but the Senior Surgical Intern was, even if temporarily, a patient, and must be humored. She forgot about the kiss immediately, anyhow, although he did not.

Her three months of probation were drawing to a close now, and her cap was already made and put away in a box, ready for the day she should don it. But she did not look at it very often.

And all the time, fighting his battle with youth and vigor, but with closed eyes, and losing it day by day, was Johnny Fraser.

Then, one night on the roof, Jane Brown had to refuse the Senior Surgical Intern. He took it very hard.

"We'd have been such pals," he said, rather wistfully, after he saw it was no use.

"We can be, anyhow."

"I suppose," he said with some bitterness, "that I'd have stood a better chance if I'd done as you wanted me to about that fellow in your ward, gone to the staff and raised hell."

"I wouldn't have married you," said Jane Brown, "but I'd have thought you were pretty much of a man."

The more he thought about that the less he liked it. It almost kept him awake that night.

It was the next day that Twenty-two had his idea. He ran true to form and carried it back to Jane Brown for her approval. But she was not enthusiastic.

"It would help to amuse them, of course, but how can you publish a newspaper without any news?" she asked, rather listlessly, for her.

"News! This building is full of news. I have some bits already. Listen!" He took a notebook out of his pocket. "The stork breaks quarantine. New baby in O ward. The chief engineer has developed a boil on his neck. Elevator Man arrested for breaking speed limit. Wanted, four square inches of cuticle for skin grafting in W. How's that? And I'm only beginning."

Jane Brown listened. Somehow, behind Twenty-two's lightness of tone, she felt something more earnest. She did not put it into words, even to herself, but she divined something new, a desire to do his bit, there in the hospital. It was, if she had only known it, a milestone in a hitherto unmarked career. Twenty-two, who had always been a man, was by way of becoming a person.

He explained about publishing it. He used to run a typewriter in college, and the convalescents could mimeograph it and sell it. There was a mimeographing machine in the office.

The Senior Surgical Intern came in just then. Refusing to marry him had had much the effect of smacking a puppy. He came back, a trifle timid, but friendly. So he came in just then and elected himself to the advertising and circulation department, and gave the Probationer the society end, although it was not his paper or his idea, and sat down at once at the table and started a limerick, commencing, *We're here in the city, marooned.*

However, he never got any further with it, because there are, apparently, no rhymes for "marooned." He refused "tuned" which several people offered him, with extreme scorn.

Up to this point, Jane Brown had been rather too worried to think about Twenty-two. She had grown accustomed to seeing him coming slowly back toward her ward, his eyes travelling much faster than he did. Not, of course, that she knew that. And to his being, in a way, underfoot a part of every day, after the Head had made rounds and was safely out of the road for a good two hours.

But two things happened that day to turn her mind in onto her heart. One was when she heard about the artificial leg. The other was when she passed the door of his room, where a large card now announced "Office of the *Quarantine Sentinel*." She passed the door, and she distinctly heard most un-hospital-like chatter within. Judging from the shadows on the glass door, too, the room was full. It sounded joyous and carefree.

Something in Jane Brown—her mind, probably—turned right around and looked into her heart, and made an odd discovery. This was that Jane Brown's heart had sunk about two inches, and was feeling very queer.

She went straight on, however, and put on a fresh collar in her little bedroom, and listed her washing and changed her shoes, because her feet still ached a lot of the time. But she was a brave person and liked to look things in the face. So before she went back to the ward, she stood in front of her mirror and said, "You're a nice nurse, Nell Brown. To talk about duty and brag about service, and then to act like a fool."

She went back to the ward and sat beside Johnny. But that night, she went up on the roof again and sat on the parapet. She could see, across the courtyard, the dim rectangles of her ward, and around a corner in plain view, room twenty-two. Its occupant was sitting at the typewriter, and working hard. Or he seemed to be. It was too far away to be sure.

Jane Brown slid down onto the roof, which was not very clean, and putting her elbows on the parapet, watched him for a long time. When he got up, at last, and came to the open window, she hardly breathed. However, he only stood there, looking toward her but not seeing her.

Jane Brown put her head on the parapet that night and cried. She thought she was crying about Johnny Fraser. She might have felt somewhat comforted had she known that Twenty-two, being tired with his day's work, had at last given way to most horrible jealousy of the Senior Surgical Intern, and that his misery was to hers as five is to one.

The first number of the *Quarantine Sentinel* was a great success. It served in the wards much the same purpose as the magazines published in the trenches. It relieved the monotony, brought the different wards together, furnished laughter and gossip.

Twenty-two wrote the editorials, published the paper, with the aid of a couple of convalescents, and in his leisure drew cartoons. He drew very well, but all his girls looked like Jane Brown. It caused a ripple of talk.

The children from the children's ward distributed them, and went back from the private rooms bearing tribute of flowers and fruit. Twenty-two himself developed a most reprehensible habit of concealing candy in the *Sentinel* office and smuggling it to his carriers. Altogether a new and neighborly feeling seemed to follow in the wake of the little paper. People who had sulked in side-by-side rooms began, in the relaxed discipline of convalescence, to pay little calls about. Crotchety dowagers knitted socks for new babies. A wave of friendliness swept over every one, and engulfed particularly Twenty-two.

In the glow of it, he changed perceptibly. This was the first popularity he had ever earned, and the first he had ever cared a fi-penny bit about. And, because he valued it, he felt more and more unworthy of it.

But it kept him from seeing Jane Brown. He was too busy for many excursions to the ward, and when he went, he was immediately the center of an animated group. He hardly ever saw her alone, and when he did, he began to suspect that she pretended duties that might have waited.

One day, he happened to go back while Doctor Willie was there, and after that, he understood her problem better.

Through it all, Johnny lived. His thin, young body was now hardly an outline under the smooth, white covering of his bed. He swallowed, faintly, such bits of liquid as were placed between his lips, but there were times when Jane Brown's fingers, more expert now, could find no pulse at all. And still she had found no way to give him his chance.

She made a last appeal to Doctor Willie that day, but he only shook his head gravely.

"Even if there was an operation now, Nellie," said Doctor Willie that day, "he could not stand it."

It was the first time that Twenty-two had known her name was Nellie.

That was the last day of Jane Brown's probation. On the next day, she was to don her cap. The *Sentinel* came out with a congratulatory editorial, and at nine o'clock that night, the First Assistant brought an announcement, in the Head's own writing, for the paper.

"The Head of the Training School announces with much pleasure the acceptance of Miss N. Jane Brown as a pupil nurse."

Twenty-two sat and stared at it for quite a long time.

That night Jane Brown fought her battle and won. She went to her room immediately after chapel, and took the family pictures off her little stand and got out ink and paper. She put the photographs out of sight, because she knew that they were counting on her, and she could not bear her mother's eyes. And then she counted her money, because she had broken another thermometer, and the ticket home was rather expensive. She had enough, but very little more.

After that she went to work.

It took her rather a long time, because she had a great deal to explain. She had to put her case, in fact. And she was not strong on either ethics or logic. She said so, indeed, at the beginning. She said also that she had talked to a lot of people, but that no one understood how she felt—that there ought to be no professional ethics, or etiquette, or anything else, where it was life or death. That she felt hospitals were to save lives and not to save feelings. It seemed necessary, after that, to defend Doctor Willie— without naming him, of course. How much good he had done, and how he came to rely on himself and his own opinion, because in the country there was no one to consult with.

However, she was not so gentle with the Staff. She said that it was standing by and letting a patient die, because it was too polite to interfere, although they had all agreed among themselves that an operation was necessary. And that if they felt that way, would they refuse to pull a child from in front of a locomotive because it was its mother's business, and she didn't know how to do it?

Then she signed it.

She turned it in at the *Sentinel* office the next morning while the editor was shaving. She had to pass it through a crack in the door. Even that, however, was enough for the editor in question to see that she wore no cap.

"But see here," he said, in a rather lathery voice, "you're accepted, you know. Where's the visible sign?"

Jane Brown was not quite sure she could speak. However, she managed.

"After you read that," she said, "you'll understand."

He read it immediately, of course, growing more and more grave, and the soap drying on his chin. Its sheer courage made him gasp.

"Good girl," he said to himself. "Brave little girl. But it finishes her here, and she knows it."

He was pretty well cut up about it, too, because while he was getting it ready, he felt as if he was sharpening a knife to stab her with. Her own knife, too. But he had to be as brave as she was.

The paper came out at two o'clock. At three, the First Assistant, looking extremely white, relieved Jane Brown of the care of H ward and sent her to her room.

Jane Brown eyed her wistfully.

"I'm not to come back, I suppose?"

The First Assistant avoided her eyes.

"I'm afraid not," she said.

Jane Brown went up the ward and looked down at Johnny Fraser. Then she gathered up her bandage scissors and her little dressing forceps and went out.

The First Assistant took a step after her, but stopped. There were tears in her eyes.

Things moved very rapidly in the hospital that day, while the guards sat outside on their camp stools and ate apples or read the newspapers, and while Jane Brown sat alone in her room.

First of all, the Staff met and summoned Twenty-two. He went down in the elevator—he had lost Elizabeth a few days before and was using a cane—ready for trouble. He had always met a fight more than halfway. It was the same instinct that had taken him to the fire.

But no one wanted to fight. The Staff was waiting, grave and perplexed, but rather anxious to put its case than otherwise. It felt misunderstood, aggrieved, and horribly afraid it was going to get in the newspapers. But it was not angry. On the contrary, it was trying its extremely intelligent best to see things from a new angle.

The Senior Surgical Intern was waiting outside. He had smoked eighteen cigarettes since he received his copy of the *Sentinel*, and was as unhappy as an intern can be.

"What the devil made you publish it?" he demanded.

Twenty-two smiled.

"Because," he said, "I have always had a sneaking desire to publish an honest paper, one where public questions can be discussed. If this isn't a public question, I don't know one when I see it."

But he was not smiling when he went in.

An hour later, Doctor Willie came in. He had brought some flowers for the children's ward, and his arms were bulging. To his surprise, accustomed as he was to the somewhat cavalier treatment of the country practitioner in a big city hospital, he was invited to the Staff room.

To the eternal credit of the Staff, Jane Brown's part in that painful half hour was never known. The Staff was careful, too, of Doctor Willie. They knew they were being irregular and were most wretchedly uncomfortable. Also, there being six of them against one, it looked rather like force, particularly since, after the first two minutes, every one of them liked Doctor Willie.

He took it so awfully well. He sat there, with his elbows on a table beside a withering mass of spring flowers, and faced the white-coated Staff, and said that he hoped he was man enough to acknowledge a mistake, and six opinions against one left him nothing else to do. The Senior Surgical Intern, who had been hating him for weeks, offered him a cigar.

He had only one request to make. There was a little girl in the training school who believed in him, and he would like to go to the ward and write the order for the operation himself.

Which he did. But Jane Brown was not there.

Late that evening the First Assistant, passing along the corridor in the dormitory, was accosted by a quiet figure in a blue uniform, without a cap.

"How is he?"

The First Assistant was feeling more cheerful than usual. The operating surgeon had congratulated her on the way things had moved that day, and she was feeling, as she often did, that, after all, work was a solace for many troubles.

"Of course, it is very soon, but he stood it well." She looked up at Jane Brown, who was taller than she was, but who always, somehow, looked rather little. There are girls like that. "Look here," she said, "you must not sit in that room and worry. Run up to the operating room and help to clear away."

She was very wise, the First Assistant. For Jane Brown went, and washed away some of the ache with the stains of Johnny's operation. Here, all about her, were the tangible evidences of her triumph, which was also a defeat. A little glow of service revived in her. If Johnny lived, it was a small price to pay for a life. If he died, she had given him his chance. The operating room nurses were very kind. They liked her courage, but they were frightened, too. She, like the others, had been right, but also, she was wrong.

They paid her tribute of little kindnesses, but they knew she must go.

It was the night nurse who told Twenty-two that Jane Brown was in the operating room. He was still up and dressed at midnight, but the sheets of tomorrow's editorial lay blank on his table.

The night nurse glanced at her watch to see if it was time for the twelve o'clock medicines.

"There's a rumor going about," she said, "that the quarantine's to be lifted tomorrow. I'll be rather sorry. It has been a change."

"Tomorrow," said Twenty-two, in a startled voice.

"I suppose you'll be going out at once?"

There was a wistful note in her voice. She liked him. He had been an oasis of cheer in the dreary rounds of the night. A very little more, and she might have forgotten her rule, which was never to be sentimentally interested in a patient.

"I wonder," said Twenty-two, in a curious tone, "if you will give me my cane?"

He was clad, at that time, in a hideous bathrobe, purchased by the orderly, over his night clothing, and he had the expression of a person who intends to take no chances.

"Thanks," said Twenty-two. "And—will you send the night watchman here?"

The night nurse went out. She had a distinct feeling that something was about to happen. At least she claimed it later. But she found the night watchman making coffee in a back pantry, and gave him her message.

Sometime later, Jane Brown stood in the doorway of the operating room and gave it a farewell look. Its white floor and walls were spotless. Shining rows of instruments on clean towels were ready to put away in the cabinets. The sterilizers glowed in warm rectangles of gleaming copper. Over all, brooded the peace of order, the quiet of the night.

Outside the operating room door, she drew a long breath, and faced the night watchman. She had left something in Twenty-two. Would she go and get it?

"It's very late," said Jane Brown. "And it isn't allowed, I'm sure."

However, what was one more rule to her who had defied them all? A spirit of recklessness seized her. After all, why not? She would never see him again. Like the operating room, she would stand in the doorway and say a mute little farewell.

Twenty-two's door was wide open, and he was standing in the center of the room, looking out. He had heard her long before she came in sight, for he too had learned the hospital habit of classifying footsteps.

He was horribly excited. He had never been so nervous before. He had made up a small speech, a sort of beginning, but he forgot it the moment he heard her, and she surprised him in the midst of trying, agonizingly, to remember it.

There was a sort of dreadful calm, however, about Jane Brown.

"The watchman says I have left something here."

It was clear to him at once that he meant nothing to her. It was in her voice.

"You did," he said. And tried to smile.

"Then, if I may have it—"

"I wish to heaven you could have it," he said, very rapidly. "I don't want it. It's darned miserable."

"It's—what?"

"It's an ache," he went on, still rather incoherent. "A pain. A misery." Then, seeing her beginning to put on a professional look: "No, not that. It's a feeling. Look here," he said, rather more slowly, "do you mind coming in and closing the door? There's a man across who's always listening."

She went in, but she did not close the door. She went slowly, looking rather pale.

"What I sent for you for is this," said Twenty-two, "are you going away? Because I've got to know."

"I'm being sent away as soon as the quarantine is over. It's—it's perfectly right. I expected it. Things would soon go to pieces if the nurses took to—took to doing what I did."

Suddenly, Twenty-two limped across the room and slammed the door shut, a proceeding immediately followed by an irritated ringing of bells at the night nurse's desk. Then he turned, his back against the door.

"Because I'm going when you do," he said, in a terrible voice. "I'm going when you go, and wherever you go. I've stood all the waiting around for a glimpse of you that I'm going to stand." He glared at her. "For weeks," he said, "I've sat here in this room and listened for you, and hated to go to sleep for fear you would pass and I wouldn't be looking through that damned door. And now I've reached the limit."

A sort of band which had seemed to be fastened around Jane Brown's head for days suddenly removed itself to her heart, which became extremely irregular.

"And I want to say this," went on Twenty-two, still in a savage tone. He was horribly frightened, so he blustered. "I don't care whether you want me or not, you've got to have me. I'm so much in love with you that it hurts."

Suddenly Jane Brown's heart settled down into a soft rhythmic beating that was like a song. After all, life was made up of love and work, and love came first.

She faced Twenty-two with brave eyes.

"I love you, too—so much that it hurts."

The gentleman across the hall, sitting up in bed, with an angry thumb on the bell, was electrified to see, on the glass door across, the silhouette of a young lady without a cap go into the arms of a very large, masculine silhouette in a dressing gown. He heard, too, the thump of a falling cane.

Late that night Jane Brown, by devious ways, made her way back to H ward. Johnny was there, a strange Johnny with a bandaged head, but with open eyes.

At dawn, the dawn of the day when Jane Brown was to leave the little world of the hospital for a little world of two, consisting of a man and a woman, the night nurse found her there, asleep, her fingers still on Johnny's thin wrist.

She did not report it.

About the Author

Dubbed the American Agatha Christie, Mary Roberts Rinehart was born in Pittsburgh in 1876. The author of more than three dozen novels, many of them best-sellers, she was also a prolific writer of plays and short stories, and several of her works were adapted for film and television. She died in New York in 1958.

To see our other great titles,
visit us at:

BLACKBIRD BOOKS
www.bbirdbooks.com

www.ingramcontent.com/pod-product-compliance
Lightning Source LLC
Chambersburg PA
CBHW020544130626
46552CB00007B/2750